Phillip & Esther

Lee

2013

REINDEER IN DIXIE

Phillip & Esther Lee

Illustrations by Molly Brooks

Carpenter's Son Publishing

"We dedicate this book to our beautiful and talented daughter Jenny, who we love very much and of which we are extremely proud."

Phillip & Esther

Reindeer in Dixie

Copyright © 2013 by Phillip and Esther Lee

Published by Carpenter's Son Publishing, Franklin, Tennessee

Published in association with Larry Carpenter of Christian Book Services, LLC
www.christianbookservices.com

Illustrations by Molly Brooks
Cover and Interior Layout Design by Suzanne Lawing
Edited by Angelle Pilkington

Printed in the United States of America

978-0-9885931-5-2

www.reindeerindixie.com.

Sugar Belle shook snowflakes from her velvety antlers. The young doe and her sister Silver Bells had been called to Santa's workshop for important news.

Sugar Belle waited patiently as Santa took a sip from a big mug of cocoa. Silver Bells tapped her hoof to the tune of "Jingle Bells."

Santa's eyes twinkled as he turned to the sisters. "I have a very special mission for two very special reindeer." He paused and smiled warmly. "How would you like to live in Nashville, Tennessee?"

Sugar Belle gasped. Silver Bells stopped her hoof-tapping right in the middle of the song.

"But...Santa..." Sugar Belle said. "Reindeer can't live in the...in the...*South*. It's too hot!"

Silver Bells stood with her mouth open, her big brown eyes unblinking.

"Ho, ho, ho!" Santa laughed and his big belly shook. "My helpers Farmer and Mrs. Lee will take care of you. You'll be the first reindeer in Dixie, and there are many children there who want to meet you. Can you be brave little reindeer?"

Reindeer should live in the cold and snowy North, not in the warm and rainy South! Sugar Belle thought. But she would never disappoint Santa. With a nod to Silver Bells, she raised her head to jolly ole Saint Nick. "We'll make you proud, Santa!"

Sugar Belle was still worried the next afternoon as the sisters watched the Lees' white truck and trailer pull up on the snow-packed North Pole path.

Be brave, Sugar Belle told herself as the Lees climbed out.

Sugar Belle bounded up to them. "Hi! I'm Sugar Belle! This is Silver Bells! We can't wait to see Tennessee!"

"Well, hello there!" Mrs. Lee said. She smiled as she helped Silver Bells into the reindeer trailer.

Farmer Lee gave Sugar Belle a tip of his cowboy hat. "It's nice to meet you, Sugar Belle. You are very brave to be the first one of Santa's reindeer to live in the South. Are you ready for the adventure?"

Sugar Belle took a deep breath. "I'm ready!"

When they finally arrived in Tennessee, the early morning sun was shining on the farmland. The farm sat atop a large knoll with hills of green stretching out in every direction. A grove of White Pine Christmas trees completed the pretty picture. "It's beautiful," Sugar Belle said softly.

Silver Bells pranced ahead as Mrs. Lee led them to their stables. Inside the huge space were several stalls lined with soft straw and the biggest fan either reindeer had ever seen. "It'll keep you cool in the warm summer months," Mrs. Lee explained.

Sugar Belle explored the stable and noticed a calendar hanging just across from her stall. It had an illustration of Santa's sleigh—with eight of her reindeer friends leading it.

Mrs. Lee came up beside her and patted the soft fur on her neck. "Welcome home, Sugar Belle."

Mrs. Lee tidied up the tack room and then turned on a radio, and Silver Bells immediately began tapping her hoof in time to the beat. "What kind of music is this?" she asked Mrs. Lee. They had, of course, only ever heard Christmas carols.

"It's country music," Mrs. Lee replied as she put out fresh hay and water.

Sugar Belle was listening to Silver Bells hum along with the twangy country singer when Farmer Lee joined them in the barn.

"I hope you two like your new home?" he asked, and the sisters nodded happily. "Well, good! You'll have time to settle in before the Christmas season and your first Reindeer in Dixie visit. There are so many people here who are excited to meet you!"

Before long, the weather turned cold and inviting, and the day of their first Reindeer in Dixie visit had finally come. Mrs. Lee brushed the sisters' coats, then put on their brand-new, bright-red halters with golden jingle bells on them.

Sugar Belle held her head high, her antlers now fully grown, as Mrs. Lee slipped the halter into place. Sugar Belle gave her head a shake and the jingle bells rang merrily.

"Jingle bells, jingle bells, jingle all the way..." Silver Bells started.

Sugar Belle was laughing as Mr. Lee joined them in the stables. "It's time to go meet your new fans!" he said.

When they arrived at the nearby Ronald McDonald house, Farmer Lee led the sisters out of the trailer. Sugar Belle's hooves made crunching sounds as she padded out onto the frosty grass. She saw a big crowd of people listening to Christmas music and drinking hot cocoa.

"Santa's reindeer are here!" shouted a little boy. His glasses were slightly askew and his cheeks were rosy as he ran over to meet Sugar Belle.

Sugar Belle stood as still as she could so she wouldn't frighten him, but he walked up and kissed Sugar Belle right on her fuzzy nose!

Sugar Belle noticed a little girl perched on a window seat inside the house. She was leaning up against a big stack of pillows and staring out at them.

Sugar Belle nudged up against Farmer Lee, and he seemed to read her thoughts. "I know, Sugar Belle. She looks sad, doesn't she?"

Sugar Belle lowered her head in response, knowing it best not to speak in front of everyone.

"The volunteers here told me her name is Jenny, " he said as they walked toward the porch. "She's very sick and can't come outside, but it was her Christmas wish to meet one of Santa's reindeer."

Sugar Belle stopped before the porch stairs and looked up. Could a reindeer climb all those steps?

16

"Do you want to try to climb them?" Farmer Lee asked Sugar Belle. He tested the steps. "They're strong, but a little slippery with this weather."

Sugar Belle put her front hooves on the bottom step. She tried to get up to the next step, but her back hooves slipped on the frosty grass and she wobbled.

Sugar Belle felt Farmer Lee's hand at her side, helping to steady her.

She grunted as she pushed her way up another two steps.

"Come on, girl," Farmer Lee said softly. "You can do it."

Sugar Belle got halfway up the stairs and was panting from the effort. She looked back up at the porch and saw Jenny smiling at her.

Santa said to be brave, Sugar Belle reminded herself.

Sugar Belle locked eyes with Jenny, and with all the strength she could muster, she staggered up to the top of the stairs.

She heard the cheers of the crowd below her. Silver Bells stomped the ground with her hoof and Mrs. Lee shouted out, "Good job, Sugar Belle!"

Farmer Lee was by her side as Sugar Belle walked to the window. Jenny, wrapped in a fuzzy robe and with a scarf covering her head, held her hand up against the glass.

As Sugar Belle came closer, she saw Jenny lean in to the window, her face almost touching the glass. Sugar Belle got as close to the window as she could. She pressed her fuzzy nose right up to the glass, nose-to-nose with Jenny.

The window fogged up, and Sugar Belle could hear Jenny laughing as she wiped the window on her side. Farmer Lee wiped the window from the outside and the two new friends could see each other again.

Jenny's smile was brighter than the Christmas Star.

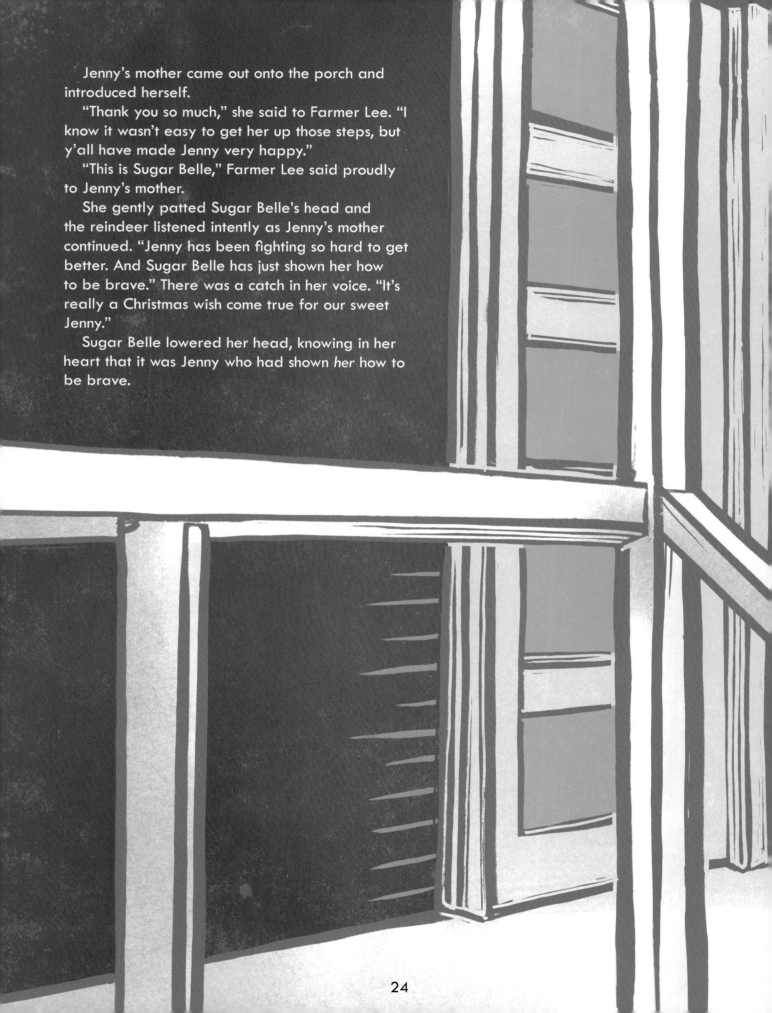

Jenny's mother came out onto the porch and introduced herself.

"Thank you so much," she said to Farmer Lee. "I know it wasn't easy to get her up those steps, but y'all have made Jenny very happy."

"This is Sugar Belle," Farmer Lee said proudly to Jenny's mother.

She gently patted Sugar Belle's head and the reindeer listened intently as Jenny's mother continued. "Jenny has been fighting so hard to get better. And Sugar Belle has just shown her how to be brave." There was a catch in her voice. "It's really a Christmas wish come true for our sweet Jenny."

Sugar Belle lowered her head, knowing in her heart that it was Jenny who had shown *her* how to be brave.

On Christmas Eve, Sugar Belle was munching on fresh hay and looking up at the picture Jenny had drawn for her. Mrs. Lee had hung the artwork right next to the Santa calendar.

Silver Bells was singing along to "Christmas in Dixie" when Sugar Belle heard sleigh bells.

Silver Bells looked out of the window of her stall. "It's Santa!" she shouted with glee.

In the blink of a reindeer's eye, Santa's sleigh landed just outside the stables. The sisters raced out to greet them, prancing and jumping with excitement.

"Ho, ho, ho!" Santa chuckled as he pulled two gifts from his big red bag. "You two have made old Santa so happy!" he said. "The Lees told me about all your good work. And a special girl named Jenny wrote me to say thank you."

Sugar Belle reared up in delight when Santa mentioned Jenny's name.

"For you, Sugar Belle," he said, "here is a reindeer flight book. This will tell you all you need to know before your first flight lesson."

The other reindeer cheered for Sugar Belle.

"And for you, Silver Bells, is a specially made reindeer guitar. Keep practicing your country music!"

Silver Bells gave a yelp. "Thank you so, so, so much, Santa!"

FLIGHT BOOK

Santa laughed again, then he straightened his jacket, and climbed back up into the beautiful red sleigh. "We haven't a moment to lose on this Christmas Eve. But I'm proud of you two. And thank goodness it's not too hot for you here in Dixie!" He winked at Sugar Belle, then gave a whistle to his team.

29

Sugar Belle watched with wonder and awe as Santa's sleigh and reindeer rose into flight. Santa gave a wave down to them. "Merry Christmas to my brave little reindeer, and to all of Dixieland!"